The Real Cat Owner's Survival Guide

Kevin Lawson

Published by Michael Pollick, 2024.

THE REAL CAT OWNER'S SURVIVAL GUIDE

First edition. August 27, 2024.

ISBN: 979-8224575978

Written by Kevin Lawson.

Table of Contents

The REAL Cat Owner's Survival Guide

Kevin Lawson

But Is It Butt-Worthy?

You know, I've been thinking a lot about the mysteries of life lately, and one of the greatest enigmas I've encountered is the behavior of cats. I mean, have you ever noticed how a cat will just casually saunter up to you, look you dead in the eye, and then present its backside like it's the most natural thing in the world? It's like they're saying, "Hey, human! Want to see my finest asset?" I can't help but wonder what's going through their little feline minds.

Picture this: you're sitting on the couch, minding your own business, perhaps scrolling through your phone or watching a show, when suddenly—BAM! Your cat decides it's time for a butt presentation. It's as if they've been practicing this move, perfecting the angle, the posture, the tail lift. It's a full-on performance, and you're the captive audience. I swear, if there were a cat Olympics, this would be a gold medal event.

Honestly, it's a bold move. I mean, if I were to walk up to someone and show them my behind, I'd probably get slapped with a restraining order. But cats? They do it with such confidence, as if they're saying, "Look at me! I'm fabulous!" And what's even more perplexing is that this isn't just a one-time thing. No, no, no. This is a ritual. They come back for encore performances. It's like they're trying to start a trend. "Hey, everyone! Butt showing is the new thing! Get on board!"

And let's talk about the timing. Why do they choose the most inappropriate moments to do this? You could be in the middle of an important Zoom call, and there it is—Mr. Whiskers, presenting his rear end to the camera like he's auditioning for a reality show. "Yes, I know you're trying to look professional, but have you seen my tail? It's magnificent!" You can almost hear the collective gasp of your coworkers. I mean, who needs a cat filter when you have an actual cat butt photobombing your meeting?

Then there's the smell factor. Oh, the smell factor. I don't know if they're aware of their own hygiene or if they just assume we'll overlook the less-than-pleasant aroma wafting from their behinds. It's like they think, "Sure, I rolled in something unspeakable yesterday, but look at this cute little wiggle!" I'm left standing there, torn between admiration for their audacity and a desperate need to open a window.

What's even funnier is the way they react after the presentation. They turn around, look at you, and then strut away as if they've just delivered the punchline of the century. "Did you see that? Did you see what I just did? You're welcome!" Meanwhile, I'm sitting there, trying to process what just happened, questioning my life choices and wondering if I should be flattered or offended.

And let's not forget the sheer absurdity of it all. Here we are, in a world filled with serious issues and existential dread, and yet, the highlight of my day is my cat's butt. It's a reminder that sometimes, life doesn't need to be taken so seriously. Sometimes, it's okay to just laugh at the ridiculousness of it all.

So, here's to our furry companions and their unapologetic butt presentations. May we all learn a thing or two from them—like how to embrace our quirks, how to strut our stuff with confidence, and, most importantly, how to find joy in the simple things. And if that means putting our behinds on display every now and then, well, maybe that's not such a bad thing after all.

https://app.videogen.io/view/brdsur

Cat Litter: Diggin' And A-Scratchin'

You ever watch a cat use a litter box? It's like observing a tiny, furry archaeologist at work, digging through layers of history with the utmost seriousness. I mean, you'd think they were unearthing some ancient treasure rather than just doing their business. There's this whole ritual involved, a performance that would make even the most seasoned Broadway actor jealous. First, the cat approaches the litter box with an air of importance, tail held high like a flag of sovereignty. You can almost hear the dramatic music playing in the background, setting the stage for what's about to unfold.

Now, here's where the magic happens. The cat hops in, and you can see the gears turning in its little brain. It squats down, and you think, "Okay, this is it. This is the moment." And then—oh, the suspense!—the cat does its thing. But it's not just any ordinary business; it's a masterpiece of nature. The sound is barely audible, almost like a whisper, as if the cat is trying to keep this whole affair a secret from the world. "Shh, don't tell anyone," it seems to say, "I'm a dignified creature, and this is just between us."

Once the deed is done, the real show begins. The cat leaps up, and for a brief moment, it surveys its work, as if assessing the quality of the output. You can almost see the pride radiating from it. "Look at what I've created!" it seems to think. But wait, the best part is yet to come. With a determined look, the cat dives back into the litter box, armed with its tiny paws, ready to bury the evidence. It's like watching a master sculptor at work, carefully crafting a mound of litter over its masterpiece. The way it digs and scratches, you'd think it was trying to unearth buried treasure rather than cover up what could only be described as a biological necessity.

And here's the kicker: the cat is so intense about this process. It's as if it believes that if it doesn't cover it up perfectly, the world will somehow come crashing down. "What if someone finds out?" it seems to ponder, frantically pawing at the litter. "What if the neighbors see? I can't let the dogs down the street know my secrets!" The urgency is palpable, and you can't help but chuckle at the sheer absurdity of it all. You've got this majestic creature, a predator that could take down a bird in a single leap, reduced to a paranoid little fluffball worried about its bathroom habits.

Now, let's talk about the technique. There's an art to burying poop, and cats have perfected it over millennia. They kick up litter like they're trying to start a sandstorm. It's not just a gentle pat here and there; oh no, this is full-on excavation. You can practically hear them saying, "If I don't bury this deep enough, I might as well have left it out in the open for everyone to see!" And they really get into it—spinning around, flinging litter everywhere, as if they're in the midst of a catnip-fueled frenzy. You'd think they were conducting a symphony, each paw movement a note in a grand composition.

Finally, after what feels like an eternity of digging, the cat stands back, surveying its work with the satisfaction of an artist unveiling a masterpiece. "Behold, my work of art!" it seems to declare, tail flicking with pride. And then, as if on cue, it struts out of the litter box like it just conquered a mountain, leaving behind a perfectly covered pile that would make any archaeologist weep with joy. It's a moment of triumph, a victory in the daily grind of cat life.

And as I watch this whole spectacle unfold, I can't help but think: if only we humans could approach our own responsibilities with half the dedication and flair that a cat shows in burying its poop.

https://app.videogen.io/view/snollc

Dispatch, We Have The Zoomies In Progress

You know, there's something utterly ridiculous about the phenomenon we've all come to know and love as "the zoomies." It's that magical moment when your otherwise dignified feline transforms into a furry tornado, a furry embodiment of chaos. One minute, they're curled up on the couch, looking like a fluffy little potato, and the next, they're hurtling through the house like a miniature rocket. You'd think they were possessed by some hyperactive spirit, but no, it's just a cat being a cat.

I mean, let's talk about the sheer absurdity of it all. One moment, they're in deep hibernation, dreaming of world domination or perhaps plotting to overthrow the dog next door, and the next, they're leaping off the furniture like an Olympic gymnast. You can practically hear the dramatic music playing in the background as they launch themselves off the couch, their little paws barely touching the ground as they become a blur of fur and enthusiasm. It's like someone hit the fast-forward button on their life, and they've suddenly decided that the living room is their personal racetrack.

And let's not forget the sound effects. Oh, the sound effects! You'd think they were training for the feline version of the Indy 500. The pitter-patter of their paws echoes through the house like a stampede of tiny elephants. It's a cacophony that could wake the dead, and yet, there's something almost endearing about it. You can't help but chuckle as they zoom past you, their eyes wide and wild, as if they've just discovered a hidden stash of catnip. In that moment, they're not just a pet; they're an athlete in the prime of their career, a furry little superstar on a quest for glory.

But where exactly are they racing to? That's the million-dollar question. Is there a finish line somewhere in the kitchen? Are they trying to catch the elusive red dot of the laser pointer that's taunted them for years? Or maybe they're just trying to assert their dominance over the living room rug, claiming it as their territory with every chaotic leap. It's as if they've suddenly decided that the house is their playground, and they're the reigning champion of the zoomies.

And then, just as suddenly as it began, it stops. One moment, you're witnessing a feline frenzy, and the next, they come to a screeching halt, panting as if they just completed a marathon. They look around, bewildered, as if they've just woken up from a dream and are trying to make sense of the chaos they've created. It's like they're thinking, "What just happened? Did I really just leap off the bookshelf? Where's my dignity?"

And here's the kicker: you can't help but laugh. You're standing there, trying to contain your amusement, but it's impossible. There's something inherently funny about a creature that's supposed to be all about grace and poise suddenly losing their marbles. It's a reminder that even the most refined beings can have their moments of sheer silliness.

You start to wonder if they're secretly judging you for your lack of enthusiasm. "Look at me, human! I can fly! Why aren't you joining me?" And you're left there, holding your coffee, half-amused and half-concerned about the state of your furniture.

So, the next time your cat gets the zoomies, just sit back and enjoy the show. Embrace the chaos. After all, it's not every day you get to witness a furry whirlwind of energy tearing through your home. It's a reminder that life is too short to take too seriously, and sometimes, you just need to let loose and run wild—preferably with a little more grace than a cat, but hey, we can't all be furry tornadoes.

https://app.videogen.io/view/nwtxgd

Rub My Belly, Take Your Chances

You know, there's something utterly ridiculous about the way cats behave, particularly when they decide to roll over and present their belly to you like it's some kind of sacred offering. It's as if they're saying, "Behold! The soft underbelly of the mighty feline!" But let's be honest here; it's less of a display of trust and more of a challenge. It's like they're daring you to engage in a game of "Will you or won't you?" with the stakes being your own dignity and a possible trip to the emergency room.

I mean, picture this: you're sitting there, minding your own business, maybe scrolling through your phone, when suddenly, your cat—let's call him Mr. Whiskers—decides it's time to flaunt his fluff. He rolls over with the grace of a drunken ballerina, legs splayed out like he's auditioning for a role in a circus. And there it is, the belly, the holy grail of cat anatomy, gleaming with the promise of softness and warmth. You can't help but think, "Oh, how cute!" But then, a little voice in the back of your head whispers, "Danger, Will Robinson! Danger!"

Now, if you're a cat person, you know the rules. You've read the manuals, watched the YouTube videos, and maybe even consulted a feline psychologist. You know that a cat's belly is not just a belly; it's a no-fly zone, a forbidden territory. It's like the cat version of Area 51. You can look, but you cannot touch. Touching is an invitation for chaos, a summons for claws and teeth to spring into action like they've been training for this moment their entire lives. But there's Mr. Whiskers, sprawled out like he's auditioning for a catnip commercial, and you're torn between the urge to rub that fluffy belly and the fear of losing a finger in the process.

So, what do you do? You sit there, staring at him, contemplating life choices. You think about how you've fed him, cleaned his litter box, and provided endless entertainment with that laser pointer. Surely, you've earned the right to give that belly a gentle scratch, right? But as you stretch your hand out, you can almost hear the ominous music playing in the background, warning you of the impending doom. It's like a scene from a horror movie: the unsuspecting hero reaches for the belly, and the audience collectively gasps, knowing full well what's about to happen.

And then, the moment of truth arrives. You touch the belly, and for a fleeting second, it feels like you've won the lottery. Mr. Whiskers purrs, and your heart swells with pride. You're the chosen one! But just as quickly, the mood shifts. His eyes narrow, and suddenly, you're on the receiving end of a furry tornado. Claws are out, and you're left wondering if you should have just settled for a simple head scratch instead.

But let's not forget the sheer audacity of these creatures. They know exactly what they're doing. It's like they've concocted a master plan to keep us on our toes, to remind us who really runs the house. They roll over, flashing that belly, and we fall for it every single time. We're like moths to a flame, helplessly drawn in, only to get burned.

So, the next time you find yourself in the presence of a belly-flopping cat, remember: it's not just a display of affection; it's a test of your resolve, a challenge to your sanity. And as you weigh your options, just know that whatever you decide, you're in for a wild ride. Because in the world of cats, nothing is ever as simple as it seems.

https://app.videogen.io/view/zldnvc

Rubbing Noses, Bonking Heads: So This Is Love

Y ou know, there's something incredibly endearing about the way cats express their affection, and I'm not talking about the gentle purring or the way they curl up on your lap. No, I'm talking about that absurd, head-bumping ritual that seems to be exclusive to our feline friends. It's as if they've taken a page out of a toddler's playbook, deciding that the best way to show love is to launch a surprise attack with their skulls. I mean, who needs a love letter when you can have a cat suddenly ramming its head into your leg like a tiny, furry battering ram?

Picture this: I'm lounging on the couch, completely engrossed in my latest binge-watch session, when out of nowhere, my cat, Sir Whiskers McFluff, decides that it's the perfect moment to demonstrate his affection. He stealthily approaches, tail high, eyes wide, and then—BAM!—he launches himself at my shin like a furry cannonball. It's like he's trying to score points in some bizarre game of feline rugby, and I'm the unsuspecting goalpost. I'm left reeling, half-laughing, half-wincing as I try to process what just happened.

And let's talk about the technique. It's not just a simple bump; it's a full-on headbutt, the kind that would make a professional football player proud. I swear, if there were a judging panel for cat headbutts, Sir Whiskers would take home the gold medal. He approaches with a determined look in his eye, as if he's about to embark on a life-changing mission. And then, with all the grace of a drunken ballet dancer, he collides with me. It's part love tap, part "I'm going to knock you off your feet," and entirely confusing.

Sometimes, I wonder if he's trying to communicate something profound. Is he saying, "I love you"? Or maybe, "Feed me"? Perhaps it's a secret cat code that only the elite members of the feline community understand. "Initiate headbutt protocol," he might be saying to himself as he gears up for the impact. But honestly, I'm left with more questions than answers. Does he think I'm a giant scratching post? Or is he just trying to assert his dominance over me, his humble human servant?

Then there are the times when he decides that my face is the best target. I'll be lying in bed, blissfully drifting off to sleep, when suddenly, I'm jolted awake by a furry missile crashing into my forehead. It's like being smacked with a soft, purring pillow, and I can't decide whether to laugh or cry. I mean, who knew that the most dangerous part of owning a cat would be the risk of a nocturnal headbutt? I can just imagine him plotting in the shadows, waiting for the perfect moment to strike, like a ninja in a fur coat.

And let's not forget the aftermath of these headbutts. There's always that moment of confusion, where I'm left wondering if I should pet him, scold him, or just laugh it off. He'll look up at me with those big, innocent eyes, as if to say, "What? I just wanted to show you some love!" And in that moment, all my frustration melts away, because how can you stay mad at a creature that believes headbutting is the highest form of affection?

So here I am, forever the target of Sir Whiskers' affection, dodging headbutts like a pro. I've learned to embrace this bizarre ritual, accepting that love comes in all forms—even if it means occasionally getting knocked over by a fluffy little cannonball. And honestly, I wouldn't have it any other way. After all, who needs a romantic partner when you have a cat that thinks you're the best thing since catnip?

https://app.videogen.io/view/kdaxsm

Is That All You Do? Bird Imitations?

You know, I've always found cats to be these fascinating little enigmas wrapped in fur. They prance around like they own the place, which, let's be honest, they probably do. But what really gets me is that odd little habit they have of chattering. You know what I mean? That peculiar sound they make when they spot a bird from the window. It's like they're trying to communicate with it, but instead sound like a malfunctioning robot trying to sing the national anthem. I mean, have you ever tried to decipher that? It's a mix of excitement, frustration, and a dash of "I wish I could fly."

So picture this: my cat, Whiskers, perched on the windowsill, eyes locked onto a sparrow that's blissfully unaware of the feline predator lurking just inches away. Whiskers starts chattering, and I swear, it sounds like he's trying to negotiate a peace treaty with the bird. "Hey, little buddy! I see you there! Let's talk about this! I promise I won't eat you... if you come a little closer." It's like he thinks he's some sort of feline diplomat. Meanwhile, the bird is probably thinking, "What is that weird noise? Is that a cat or a malfunctioning blender?"

And let's not forget the sheer variety of sounds that come out of a cat's mouth. One moment it's a chirp, the next it's a growl, and then it morphs into this bizarre combination of both. I half expect Whiskers to break out into a full-on opera. "Oh, sweet sparrow, why must you fly away? I long to taste your feathers, but alas, I am but a humble cat!" Seriously, if there were a cat talent show, Whiskers would take home the gold for best dramatic performance.

But here's the kicker: I've started to wonder if he's actually talking to me. I mean, we've had our fair share of conversations, albeit one-sided. I sit on the couch, and he jumps up next to me, looking all regal and demanding. "Meow!" he says, and I can't help but respond, "Yes, Whiskers, what is it?" And then he goes off on this whole tirade, chattering away like he's sharing the secrets of the universe. I nod along, pretending to understand, while he's probably just telling me about his latest conquest against the elusive red dot from the laser pointer.

Sometimes I think he's just trying to get me to join in on the fun. "Come on, human! You've got to try this! Just look at that bird! It's right there! Why aren't you chattering?" And I'm sitting there, thinking, "Whiskers, I'm a grown adult. I can't just start chattering at birds. What would the neighbors think?" But then again, maybe they'd join in too. A whole neighborhood of people standing by their windows, chattering at birds like it's the latest craze. "Hey, did you hear about the new bird chattering club? It's all the rage!"

And then there are those moments when he's chattering in his sleep. I'll wake up in the middle of the night to this weird symphony of sounds, and I'm convinced he's dreaming about being the king of the cat kingdom, negotiating treaties with birds and squirrels. "No, no, Mr. Squirrel, you can't just take the acorns! We had a deal!" I can't help but chuckle at the thought.

In the end, I've come to accept that Whiskers is not just a cat; he's a philosopher, a diplomat, and possibly even a comedian. He's here to remind me that life doesn't always have to be serious. Sometimes, it's about chattering at the birds and dreaming big, even if it sounds ridiculous. So here's to the cats out there, chattering away, sharing their thoughts in a language only they understand, and making us laugh in the process.

https://app.videogen.io/view/zydzmh

This New Thing Cannot Remain

You know, I've always heard that jealousy is a human emotion, a complex cocktail of insecurity and desire, but let me tell you, my cat has taken that notion and turned it into an Olympic sport. I mean, if there were medals for jealousy, my feline would be draped in gold, silver, and a few questionable bronze medals that she probably stole from the neighbor's yard. It's a full-time job for her, and frankly, I'm starting to think she deserves a raise.

Let's start with the obvious: the moment I bring home anything new. A new blanket? Oh, you'd think I just introduced a rival into our home. There's this immediate shift in the atmosphere, like I've just announced I'm running off to join the circus. She'll stalk the new item with a mixture of suspicion and disdain, her tail twitching like a metronome set to "annoyed." I swear, if she could speak, she'd be saying, "What is this? A new throne for my kingdom? You think I'm going to sit on that? Ha! As if!"

And don't even get me started on the dog next door. I can't tell if she's more jealous of the dog's existence or the fact that I sometimes pet it. The other day, I made the grave mistake of giving the dog a scratch behind the ears. My cat, who was lounging on the windowsill like a furry queen surveying her domain, suddenly leaped down with the grace of a ballerina and proceeded to knock over a potted plant. I looked at her, bewildered, and she just stared back, as if to say, "This is your fault. You brought this upon yourself."

Then there's the time I brought home a second cat. Oh boy, that was a masterclass in jealousy. I thought, "How sweet! They'll be best friends!" But no, my cat took one look at the newcomer, and it was as if I had just introduced her to her arch-nemesis. The new cat was all wide-eyed innocence, while my cat transformed into a furry little demon, hissing and swatting at the air as if she was defending her territory from an invading army. I mean, she was practically auditioning for a horror movie. I half expected her to start chanting, "There can only be one!"

And let's not forget the classic "lap battle." This is where she really shines. If I dare to sit down with my laptop, my cat will suddenly become a furry avalanche, launching herself onto my lap as if to say, "Excuse me, human, but this lap is now officially reserved for the one and only." She'll plop down, her weight perfectly calibrated to ensure that I can't move without causing a minor earthquake. If I even think about shifting my attention to the screen, she'll give me that look—the one that says, "You're not seriously going to ignore me, are you? I've just sacrificed my personal space for you, and you repay me with a glowing box? How rude!"

And let's address the "stranger danger" phase. Whenever I have guests over, my cat becomes the ultimate gatekeeper. She'll sit at the entrance of the room, giving a side-eye that could curdle milk. You'd think she was the bouncer of a high-end club, checking IDs and deciding who's worthy of her presence. If anyone dares to approach me, she'll leap into action, weaving between my legs and meowing in a tone that sounds suspiciously like, "Hey, buddy, back off! This human is mine! I don't care if you brought snacks; I was here first!"

Honestly, it's exhausting. I never signed up for this level of emotional drama. I just wanted a pet, not a furry soap opera star. But here we are, living in a world where a cat's jealousy is the leading cause of chaos in my home. I suppose I should be flattered, in a way. After all, it's nice to be so adored, even if it comes with a side of hissing and a few broken flower pots.

https://app.videogen.io/view/mlenhc

The Art Form That Is Cat Napping

Cats are the ultimate masters of napping, and their ability to find the most absurdly small spaces to curl up in is nothing short of a miracle. I mean, have you ever seen a cat squeeze itself into a box that's clearly three sizes too small? It's like watching a magician perform a trick, except instead of pulling a rabbit out of a hat, they're somehow folding their entire body into a shoebox. You've got to give them credit for their flexibility, but really, it raises the question: what is it about small spaces that makes cats think, "Ah, yes, this is the perfect spot for a snooze"?

Take my cat, Whiskers. He's a hefty little guy, not exactly the poster child for feline agility, yet he has this uncanny ability to turn into a contortionist when he spots a cozy nook. I once watched him climb into a cardboard box that was meant for a pair of shoes. I stood there, mouth agape, as he squished himself in, paws splayed out, and somehow managed to fit. It was as if he was channeling his inner origami artist, folding himself into a shape that defied the laws of physics. I half-expected him to emerge with a tiny hat and a bowtie, ready for a formal event.

And then there's the laundry basket. Oh, the laundry basket. It's like a five-star hotel for cats. Whiskers will leap into that thing, and suddenly it's like he's found the softest, warmest cloud in the universe. But here's the kicker: he doesn't just lie down. No, he has to dig himself in, burrowing deeper and deeper until he's completely hidden. You'd think he was preparing for a winter hibernation rather than a quick nap. I can't help but wonder if he thinks he's camouflaging himself, like some kind of furry ninja. "If I can't see you, you can't see me," he seems to be saying, while I'm left wondering how I can possibly do laundry with a cat in residence.

And then there are the truly bizarre choices. The other day, I found him napping inside a plastic bag. A plastic bag! I mean, what's next? A nap in the toaster? I can just picture it: "Whiskers, what are you doing?" "Just getting my beauty sleep, Mom! This is the latest trend in cat napping." It's like he's trying to prove a point: "You humans think you need a comfy bed? Pfft! I'll show you how to nap like a pro."

It's almost as if they have a secret society dedicated to finding the smallest, most inconvenient places to sleep. You can imagine them holding meetings: "Alright, team, today's objective is to find the tiniest spot possible. Bonus points if it's somewhere you're not supposed to be!" The members would nod sagely, each already plotting their next napping adventure, while the humans look on in utter confusion.

And let's not forget about the sound effects. Cats have this unique ability to make the most ridiculous noises while they're napping. You'll hear a series of snorts, purrs, and the occasional high-pitched squeak, and you can't help but think, "What are you dreaming about? A field of catnip? A never-ending supply of tuna?" It's like they're living in a parallel universe where everything is just as absurd as their choice of napping spots.

In the end, I suppose it's all part of their charm. Cats have this magical way of turning the mundane into the extraordinary. They remind us that sometimes, it's perfectly acceptable to squeeze ourselves into a tiny box, ignore the world around us, and just take a nap. So, here's to cats and their ridiculous napping habits. May they continue to defy the odds, one cramped space at a time.

https://app.videogen.io/view/rbqeyr

Chewing The Scenery, Going For The Oscar

You know, there's something truly majestic about the way a cat waits to be fed. I mean, if you've ever owned a cat, you know exactly what I'm talking about. It's like watching a masterclass in patience, or perhaps more accurately, a masterclass in manipulation. There's my cat, Sir Whiskers McPaws, perched regally on the kitchen counter, a furry little monarch surveying his kingdom. He's not just waiting for food; oh no, this is a carefully orchestrated performance.

At first, he'll casually stretch, arching his back like a yoga instructor who's just discovered the joys of downward-facing dog. He'll then glance at me with those big, innocent eyes, the kind that could make a rock weep. It's as if he's saying, "Oh, dear human, how could you possibly forget that I am a creature of the utmost importance? Surely, you must know I am starving!" Of course, I'm pretty sure he just had a three-course meal of kibble ten minutes ago, but who's counting?

Then comes the pacing. Oh, the pacing! He'll stroll from the food bowl to the pantry, back to the food bowl, and then, just for dramatic effect, he'll stop and sit down right in front of me, looking up with that "You're going to feed me, right?" expression. It's like he's auditioning for a role in a soap opera. "Will she feed him? Will she forget his royal feast? Tune in next time for the thrilling conclusion!"

But wait, there's more! The moment I dare to reach for the bag of cat food, it's as if a switch flips inside him. Suddenly, he's transformed from a dignified feline into a furry tornado. He'll dart back and forth, weaving between my legs, nearly tripping me as I attempt to open the bag. I half-expect him to start chanting, "Feed me, Seymour!" like some sort of deranged plant from a musical. Honestly, if I didn't know better, I'd think he was auditioning for a role in "Cats."

Once the food is finally poured into the bowl, you'd think I'd just dropped the crown jewels. Sir Whiskers doesn't just eat; he devours. There's a certain elegance in the way he lunges for the kibble, as if he's a lion on the savannah, taking down a gazelle. He'll shove his face into the bowl with such enthusiasm that I'm surprised he doesn't end up wearing half of it. I watch in awe as he crunches away, a mix of pride and horror washing over me. "This is what I've created," I think. "A tiny, furry vacuum cleaner with a flair for the dramatic."

And let's not forget that after the meal, there's always the obligatory grooming session. He'll sit back, licking his paws with the nonchalance of a cat who just conquered a buffet. It's as if he's saying, "Ah yes, this is the life. I eat, I groom, I nap. Rinse and repeat." Meanwhile, I'm left standing there, wondering if I'm actually the one in charge or if I've just become an unpaid servant in this feline kingdom.

So here I am, watching the aftermath of this grand performance, feeling a mix of amusement and exasperation. I can't help but laugh at the absurdity of it all. My cat, with all his regal posturing and theatrical antics, has turned a simple act of feeding into a full-blown production. And I, the unwitting audience, can't help but applaud. Because at the end of the day, who needs Netflix when you have a cat?

https://app.videogen.io/view/rdghrg

These Teeth Were Made For Chewing

You know, I've always heard that cats are these majestic creatures, revered in ancient civilizations, and adored by millions. But let's be honest here: they're also furry little tyrants with a penchant for chewing on the most bizarre things. I mean, who knew that a cat could turn into a furry vacuum cleaner with a taste for the random? It's like they have a secret mission to chew through every household item that doesn't actually belong to them.

Take my cat, Whiskers, for example. Whiskers is not just any ordinary cat; he's a connoisseur of chaos. His palate is refined, yet utterly ridiculous. I can't tell you how many times I've caught him gnawing on a pair of my favorite shoes. I mean, really? Did he mistake them for gourmet cat treats? I can just imagine him thinking, "Ah yes, the leather is aged to perfection, with just a hint of foot odor for that extra kick." And then there's the time he decided that my phone charger was the perfect late-night snack. I woke up to the sound of frantic chewing, and there he was, blissfully munching away, as if he were indulging in a five-star meal. I had to wrestle it from his jaws like a scene out of a horror movie, and let me tell you, he was not happy about it.

But it doesn't stop there. Whiskers has a knack for selecting the most random items to chew on. He once went for my hairbrush. I walked into the bathroom, and there he was, looking like a furry little gremlin, gnawing on the bristles with such enthusiasm that I half-expected him to start purring in a gourmet restaurant. "Ah yes, the synthetic fibers really bring out the flavor!" I could hear him saying. I mean, who knew that a cat could have such a diverse palate?

And let's talk about my houseplants. You'd think they were a buffet laid out just for him. I've lost count of how many times I've walked in to find him happily chomping on a succulent, as if he were at an all-you-can-eat salad bar. I can only imagine what goes through his mind: "Mmm, the crunchy leaves, the earthy taste... this is what dreams are made of!" I've tried everything—bitter sprays, moving the plants out of reach, even putting up tiny signs that say "Do Not Eat!" But nothing deters him. He just looks at me, head cocked to the side, as if to say, "You think that's going to stop me? Please."

And then there's the paper. Oh, the paper! Whiskers has developed an obsession with chewing on anything that resembles a sheet of paper. Bills, receipts, grocery lists—nothing is safe. I once found him munching on an important document, and I swear, he looked me dead in the eye as if to say, "You should've printed it on catnip paper, my friend." I mean, who knew that my cat had such a strong stance against financial responsibility?

What's truly baffling is that despite all this chewing, he has a perfectly good selection of toys. You know, the ones that are specifically designed for cats? But no, those toys are clearly inferior. They lack the thrill of danger that comes with chewing on a forbidden object. It's as if he's saying, "Why play with a mouse toy when I can chew on your important documents and ruin your day?"

So here's to you, Whiskers, the furry little chaos agent. May your chewing adventures continue, and may you never run out of random things to chew on. Just remember, if you ever decide to take a bite out of my couch, we might have a problem. But until then, keep living your best life, one random chew at a time.

https://app.videogen.io/view/tucgyp

If It Fits, I Sits. You Got A Problem With That?

You know, there's something about cats and boxes that just defies all logic. I mean, we're talking about a creature that has the entire world at its paws—soft couches, warm beds, sunbeams streaming through windows—and yet, it chooses to spend hours, days even, in a cardboard box. It's like they've stumbled upon the ultimate treasure, and we're all just too dense to understand it. I can't help but wonder if there's some ancient cat wisdom that we humans have completely overlooked. Maybe they've cracked the code to happiness, and it's all about finding the perfect box.

Let's start with the sheer variety of boxes available. You've got your standard shipping box, which is basically the feline equivalent of a five-star hotel. It's spacious, it's sturdy, and it's got that delightful crinkly sound that's music to a cat's ears. Then there are the smaller boxes, the ones that look like they were designed for a pair of socks but are somehow the perfect fit for a cat that weighs ten pounds. It's like watching a magician pull a rabbit out of a hat—how do they do it? One minute, there's a box, and the next, there's a cat crammed inside, looking at you like you're the crazy one.

And let's not forget about the novelty boxes. You know the ones I'm talking about—the ones that come with the latest gadget or the subscription box you ordered on a whim. The moment you crack that box open, your cat is there, ready to claim it as their new kingdom. It doesn't matter what's inside; the box itself is the prize. I swear, if cats had a currency, it would be boxes. "I'll trade you three shoeboxes for that fancy catnip toy."

Now, you might think it's just a phase, something they'll grow out of, but no. This obsession is lifelong. My cat, Whiskers—who, by the way, has never met a box he didn't like—has a special relationship with every box in the house. He has his favorites, of course. The Amazon box is a classic, but there's also that one box that used to hold a fancy bottle of wine. I don't know what it is about that box, but it's like a cat magnet. The moment I bring it in, it's like I've summoned the spirit of all the cats that have ever lived. Whiskers leaps into it with such enthusiasm that you'd think I'd just handed him a winning lottery ticket.

And the way they get in! It's like a performance art piece. They approach the box with this cautious curiosity, tail twitching, eyes wide. Then, suddenly, they launch themselves into it, all limbs flailing, as if they're trying to break the sound barrier. And if the box is too small? No problem! They'll contort themselves into a shape that defies all laws of physics. I've seen Whiskers fit into a box that was clearly meant for a pair of shoes. I don't know how he does it, but he emerges triumphant, like a cat magician revealing his latest trick.

But here's the kicker: when you take the box away, it's like you've committed the ultimate betrayal. Whiskers will stare at me with this look of utter disappointment, as if I've just told him that Santa isn't real. "How could you?" his eyes say. "You've taken my fortress, my sanctuary!" It's a heart-wrenching moment, really. I half expect him to pack his tiny suitcase and leave home in protest.

So, what's the lesson here? Maybe it's that happiness doesn't come from the big things in life. Maybe it's about finding joy in the simplest of pleasures, like a cardboard box. Or maybe, just maybe, cats are onto something we humans are still trying to figure out. After all, in a world full of chaos, isn't it comforting to know that all you really need is a good box and a little imagination?

https://app.videogen.io/view/wuqgqx

Just The Half Of A Thing I Need, How Nice?

You know, there's something truly special about the relationship between cats and their owners. It's a bond that transcends mere companionship; it's a master-and-servant dynamic wrapped in a fluffy, purring package. And if you've ever had the delightful experience of being gifted by your cat, you know exactly what I'm talking about. It's like receiving a present from a toddler who just discovered the concept of giving, but instead of macaroni art, you get a half-chewed mouse. Yes, that's right, your beloved feline has decided to express their affection in the most endearing way possible—by bringing you gifts.

Now, let's be honest here: when you first adopt a cat, you envision cuddles, playful antics, and the occasional cat video-worthy moment. You don't quite picture yourself standing in the middle of your living room, horrified, as your cat drops a "gift" at your feet. The first time it happened to me, I thought I was being pranked. I mean, who knew my little fluffball was moonlighting as a hunter? I had always assumed they were more into napping and knocking things off tables. But there it was, a small, lifeless creature, a token of their "affection," as if to say, "Look, human! I've provided for you! Aren't you proud?"

At first, I was flattered. My cat, whom I affectionately named Sir Purrs-a-Lot, clearly thought I was incapable of hunting for myself. "What a thoughtful little creature," I mused. But then the reality of the situation sank in. Sir Purrs-a-Lot was not just being considerate; he was trying to teach me a lesson. "You think you can just sit on the couch all day, scrolling through your phone? Think again! You need to learn how to fend for yourself!" I could almost hear him saying, his tail flicking with a hint of disdain.

The gifts kept coming. One day, it was a lizard, another day, a bird. I began to feel like I was living in a wildlife documentary, where the narrator would say, "And here we see the domestic cat, bringing its owner the spoils of its hunt, completely oblivious to the fact that the human is rather horrified." I mean, I appreciate the effort, but I didn't sign up for a lesson in survival skills. I didn't want to learn how to gut a rodent; I just wanted to enjoy my Netflix binge in peace!

And let's not forget the sheer variety of gifts. Sir Purrs-a-Lot has an impressive collection. There's the occasional sock, which I'm convinced he thinks is a small animal. And then there's the infamous "gift" that was a half-eaten piece of cat food. Yes, you heard that right. My cat brought me a gift of his own food, as if to say, "Look, I'm sharing! Aren't you lucky?" I was left standing there, wondering if I should be touched or disgusted.

I've come to accept that this is just part of the cat-owner experience. It's like having a toddler who thinks you need to be reminded how to eat. Every time Sir Purrs-a-Lot drops another "gift," I try to remind myself that it's the thought that counts. And maybe, just maybe, this is his way of saying he loves me. It's his version of a love letter—albeit a rather gruesome one.

So, here's to our furry friends and their bizarre gift-giving rituals. They may not be the most conventional presents, but they come with a certain charm. Just remember to keep a trash bag handy and a sense of humor at the ready because, in the world of cats, every day is a surprise party—complete with the occasional dead critter.

https://app.videogen.io/view/tkvmrq

Feline Indifference: Are You Still Here?

You know, I've come to a startling conclusion about my cat. I think she's a professional at ignoring me. I mean, it's almost like she's got a PhD in feline disregard. I've seen her do it time and time again, and honestly, I'm starting to feel like I'm in a one-sided relationship with a furry diva who's just too good for my attention. I walk into the room, and there she is, perched on her favorite windowsill, gazing out at the world as if she's auditioning for the role of the world's most disinterested observer. I swear, if she could roll her eyes, she would do it with such flair that it would put any teenage girl to shame.

"Hey, Luna!" I call out, waving my arms like a circus performer trying to catch the attention of a disinterested elephant. Nothing. Not even a flick of her tail. It's as if I've just announced that I'm serving broccoli for dinner. I could be offering her the finest gourmet tuna, and she wouldn't even bother to turn her head. I could be standing there, arms full of catnip toys, and she'd still be more interested in the dust motes dancing in the sunlight. It's like I'm speaking a foreign language, and she's chosen to be fluent in "I don't care."

I've tried everything to get her attention. I've resorted to the classic "crinkle the treat bag" tactic, which usually works like a charm. But not with Luna. No, she's seen through my ruse. She'll glance over, give me a look that says, "You think I'm falling for that? Please," and then return her focus to the outside world, where the birds are chirping and the squirrels are plotting their next great escape. I'm convinced she's got a secret alliance with them. "Hey, if you see my owner coming, just keep acting cute and I'll ignore her for the rest of the day," she probably tells them.

And then there are the times I try to engage her in play. I pull out the feather wand, the laser pointer, the crinkly ball that's supposed to send her into a frenzy of feline excitement. I wave it around like I'm trying to summon a spirit from the beyond. But no, she just yawns, stretches, and looks at me as if I've just suggested we go for a jog together. I mean, really? Jog? For a cat, that's the equivalent of asking a human to run a marathon while wearing a tutu.

I've even tried the "I'll ignore you back" strategy, thinking maybe if I just pretend she doesn't exist, she'll come running to me like a lost child. But no, she's not fazed. She'll just settle in for a nice long nap, purring softly, as if to say, "You think you can ignore me? I'm the queen of this castle, and I'll nap as long as I want."

And let's not even get started on the moments when I'm actually busy, like on a work call or deep into a project. That's when she decides it's prime time to walk across my keyboard or sit right in front of my monitor, blocking my view as if to say, "Oh, you're busy? That's adorable. But have you seen me? I'm fabulous!"

So here I am, the devoted servant to a creature who has mastered the art of indifference. I've accepted my role as the cat's personal assistant, forever at her beck and call, but only when she actually feels like it. It's a humbling experience, really. I've learned that love can be one-sided, and sometimes the best you can do is just sit back and enjoy the view of your cat living her best life, completely uninterested in yours.

https://app.videogen.io/view/oencim

World Staring Contest Champions Since Forever

You ever find yourself in a staring contest with your cat? I mean, you think you're just sitting there, minding your own business, maybe scrolling through your phone, and then you feel it. That intense gaze, like lasers boring into your soul. You look over, and there it is: your cat, perched like a furry sphinx, eyes wide and unblinking, just staring at you. And suddenly, you're thrust into this bizarre duel of wills. It's you versus the feline overlord, and let me tell you, the stakes are high. Who knew that somewhere in the universe, there was a cosmic scoreboard keeping track of these things?

At first, you think, "This will be easy. I'm a human. I have the power of rational thought, the ability to blink, and I definitely have the advantage of being able to change the channel on the TV." But no, your cat has other plans. That little fluffball is a master of zen. You blink, and it's like your cat is silently judging you, saying, "Pathetic." You try to regain your composure, but the longer you stare, the more you feel like you're staring into the abyss—and let me tell you, the abyss has whiskers.

And then there's the moment when you start to feel the pressure. The cat's eyes are like two glowing orbs of determination, and you're just sitting there, thinking about how ridiculous this whole situation is. I mean, who would've thought that my afternoon would be consumed by a staring contest with a creature that spends 16 hours a day sleeping? But here we are, two competitors locked in a battle of wills, and I can't help but wonder what's going on in that furry little head. Is it plotting world domination? Or just contemplating the meaning of life, which, for a cat, probably boils down to "Where's my next meal?"

I try to distract myself. I glance at my phone, scroll through social media, maybe even check the latest cat memes—oh, the irony. But no, my cat remains steadfast, unmoved by the digital distractions. It's like it knows I'm trying to cheat. It's almost as if it's saying, "You think you can outsmart me with your funny pictures and videos? Please. I'm the one who knocks over your glass of water at 3 AM just because I can."

And then, just when I think I might be gaining the upper hand, the cat does something utterly infuriating. It tilts its head slightly, as if to say, "Oh, you think you're winning? Watch this." And it starts to blink, slowly, dramatically, like it's performing some sort of feline magic trick. I'm convinced that it's trying to hypnotize me. I blink back, but it's like I'm caught in a trance. I can feel my eyelids getting heavier, and I wonder if I'm going to end up in some sort of cat-induced coma.

Finally, I can't take it anymore. I break the gaze, and the cat immediately perks up, tail flicking with triumph. "I knew I'd win," it seems to say, as it struts away, tail held high like a flag of victory. I'm left sitting there, defeated by a creature that thinks a good day is defined by how many sunbeams it can nap in. I can't help but laugh at the absurdity of it all. I mean, here I am, a grown adult, bested by a creature that spends half its life grooming itself and the other half plotting its next nap.

And yet, as I watch my cat saunter off, I can't help but feel a strange sense of camaraderie. We're both just trying to navigate this bizarre existence, one staring contest at a time. Maybe next time, I'll be ready. Maybe I'll even train for it. But deep down, I know the truth: in the end, the cat always wins.

https://app.videogen.io/view/zydlxa

I Feel The Knead, The Knead For Biscuits

You know, there's something utterly ridiculous about having a cat. I mean, who decided that we would be the ones to serve these furry little tyrants? It's like we signed up for a lifetime of servitude without even reading the fine print. And speaking of fine print, let's talk about the kneading. You know that adorable little behavior where your cat pummels your lap as if it's auditioning for a role in a feline version of "Fight Club"? Yeah, that's what I'm talking about.

So there I was, minding my own business, trying to enjoy a peaceful afternoon with a cup of tea and a book. Suddenly, my cat, Mr. Whiskers – and I swear, he thinks he's royalty – decides that my lap is the perfect place for his workout. He hops up, looks me dead in the eye, and starts kneading like he's preparing dough for a gourmet pizza. And let me tell you, the only thing rising is my blood pressure.

At first, it's kind of cute. I mean, who doesn't love a cat that wants to show affection? But then, as he digs his claws into my thighs like he's trying to find the hidden treasure of catnip, I start to question my life choices. I can almost hear him thinking, "Ah, yes, this is the spot. Right here, where the skin is the most tender. Perfect for my little kneading session!" I can't help but wonder if he's secretly plotting to turn me into a human pancake.

And let's not forget the purring. Oh, the purring! It's like an engine revving up, and you think it's all sweet and soothing until you realize it's just a warning signal. "Beware, human! I'm about to turn you into a scratching post!" You know that moment when you're trying to relax, and then suddenly, you're thrust into a chaotic game of 'how much pressure can I take before I scream?' It's like being in a weird massage parlor run by a sadistic cat. "Would you like the knead and claw special today, or should I just go for the full-on surprise attack?"

And then there's the aftermath. Once Mr. Whiskers is done with his workout, he flops down, satisfied, as if he's just conquered Everest. Meanwhile, I'm left with the imprints of his little paws all over my legs, like a bizarre cat-themed tattoo. I look down at my thighs, and it's like I've been through a battle. "Ah, yes, the marks of a true cat servant," I think to myself, as I start to contemplate whether I should add "cat kneader" to my resume.

But the best part? The best part is when you think you've finally escaped the kneading session, only to have him return for an encore. It's like a bad relationship where they keep coming back for more. You're sitting there, enjoying a moment of peace, and then bam! He's back, ready to unleash the kneading fury once again. It's as if he's saying, "Did you really think I was done? Oh, sweet, naive human. You'll never be free of my knead-y love!"

And honestly, I can't be too mad at him. I mean, who can resist that face? The little twitch of his whiskers, the way his eyes close in pure bliss as he kneads into my lap like it's the best thing since sliced bread. It's hard to stay annoyed when you're staring at a creature so blissfully unaware of the chaos he causes. In the end, I realize that this is just part of the deal when you invite a cat into your life. You trade your lap for a little love, a little chaos, and a lot of kneading. And honestly, I wouldn't have it any other way. Well, maybe with a little less clawing. But still, I'm pretty sure that's just part of the charm.

https://app.videogen.io/view/bhnpog

A Lick And No Promise

You know, there's something utterly absurd about the way cats express their affection. I mean, here I am, a fully grown adult, and I have this furry little creature that I've decided to share my life with. And what does this creature do to show its love? It licks me. Yes, you heard that right. My cat, with all the grace of a tiny, furry tornado, decides that my arm, my face, or sometimes even my toes, is the perfect canvas for its grooming artistry. It's like I'm a living, breathing ice cream cone, and my cat is the world's most determined, if slightly misguided, dessert enthusiast.

Let's break this down. Cats are supposed to be these regal, dignified beings, right? They strut around like they own the place, which, to be fair, they do. But then, out of nowhere, they launch into this licking frenzy. It's like they've mistaken me for a giant cat treat. I can't help but wonder, what goes through their minds? Do they think I'm dirty? Is my skin somehow lacking in the proper cat flavor? I mean, I shower regularly, but clearly, my cat has a different standard of cleanliness. Maybe I should start taking notes from it. "Oh, you just licked my elbow for the third time today? Thanks! I'll add that to my self-care routine!"

And let's talk about the technique. It's not just a casual lick here and there; it's a full-on grooming session. I'm sitting there, minding my own business, maybe enjoying a snack or trying to read a book, and suddenly, I'm hit with the rough, sandpaper tongue of my feline friend. It's like being exfoliated by a very enthusiastic, very persistent little creature. I'd pay a fortune for a spa day that felt half as thorough, but instead, I'm stuck on my couch, trying to dodge the onslaught of cat saliva while simultaneously wondering if I should be flattered or horrified.

And the timing! Oh, the timing is impeccable. You know that moment when you've just settled down for a nice meal, perhaps something that smells delicious, and suddenly, there's a cat on your lap, staring at you with those big, pleading eyes? You think, "Oh, sweet little furball, I'll share a bite." But before you know it, that same furball has decided that your hand is the perfect spot for a grooming session, right as you're about to take a bite of your sandwich. There's nothing quite like the sensation of a cat tongue on your fingers, especially when you're trying to enjoy a bite of turkey and Swiss. It's like a bizarre culinary experience, where the main course is suddenly garnished with a sprinkle of cat drool. Bon appétit!

And then there's the aftermath. After a good licking, my arm looks like it's been through a battle. There are little wet spots everywhere, and I can't help but feel like I need to explain myself to anyone who walks in. "Oh, no, don't mind the cat saliva; it's just a sign of affection!" I mean, how do you even justify that? It's not like I can put it on my resume: "Excellent interpersonal skills, proficient in cat communication, and experienced in handling unexpected licking incidents."

But here's the kicker: despite all the chaos, the licking, the drooling, and the awkward moments, I wouldn't trade it for anything. It's a strange, bizarre love language that only cat owners understand. When that little creature decides to lick me, it's a reminder that I'm not just a human in its territory; I'm part of its world. And honestly, if that means being a giant, furry popsicle every now and then, I guess I'm okay with that. Because in the end, who doesn't want to be loved, even if it comes with a side of cat drool?

https://app.videogen.io/view/mmuwtk

Running Faucets And Cats: What's A Utility Bill?

You know, there's something utterly fascinating about watching a cat drink water from a tap. I mean, if you haven't seen it, you're missing out on a slice of life that's both hilarious and oddly philosophical. Picture this: you're just minding your own business, maybe scrolling through your phone, when suddenly, out of the corner of your eye, you spot your cat. There it is, perched like a furry little deity, staring at the tap as if it's just discovered the meaning of life.

Now, let's break this down. Cats are notoriously finicky creatures. They'll sniff at their food as if it's a gourmet dish gone wrong, yet when it comes to water, they suddenly develop an air of connoisseurship. They'll turn their noses up at a perfectly good bowl of water—filtered, room temperature, the works—but let a drop of running water hit their radar, and it's like they've found the Fountain of Youth. The moment that tap turns on, it's like the cat's personal signal to enter full-on Olympic athlete mode.

I mean, have you seen how they leap? One moment they're lounging on the couch, looking like a fluffy potato, and the next, they're a blur of fur, launching themselves toward the sink. It's as if they've been training for this moment their entire lives. They land with a grace that defies all laws of physics, and suddenly it's like a scene from a nature documentary. "Here we see the domestic cat, the apex predator, in its natural habitat, stalking the elusive water source."

And then, the drinking begins. There's a ritualistic quality to it. First, they approach the tap with an air of skepticism, as if they're about to negotiate a peace treaty. They sniff at the faucet, giving it a thorough inspection, because heaven forbid they drink from anything that hasn't been properly vetted. Once they've deemed it worthy, they begin their delicate dance. Their tongues flick out with a precision that would make a seasoned sushi chef jealous. It's a mesmerizing spectacle, really. They lap at the water, and for a fleeting moment, you might think you're witnessing some kind of art performance. "Behold! The Cat and the Tap: A Love Story."

But here's where it gets really funny. The cat, in all its wisdom, seems to forget that it's not a fish. It's not designed for aquatic living. So, as it's lapping away, it inevitably gets a little too excited. Water splashes everywhere—on the counter, on the floor, and if you're lucky, on you. It's like a mini water park in your kitchen, and your cat is the main attraction, completely oblivious to the chaos it's causing. You're left standing there, half laughing, half exasperated, wondering if you should intervene or just let nature take its course.

And let's not forget the aftermath. After a good, hearty drink, your cat struts away, tail held high, as if it's just conquered Mount Everest. There's a certain swagger to its walk, a proud acknowledgment of its hydration achievement. Meanwhile, you're left to mop up the mini lake that has formed in your kitchen. You can't help but chuckle at the absurdity of it all. Here's this creature, so refined in its elegance, yet it can't manage to drink water without turning your home into a splash zone.

So, the next time you see your cat eyeing that tap, just remember: it's not just about hydration. It's a performance, a spectacle, a reminder that even in the mundane act of drinking water, there's a world of hilarity waiting to unfold. And honestly, who needs a reality show when you have a cat and a tap? Just sit back, grab some popcorn, and enjoy the show.

https://app.videogen.io/view/oprksg

You Saw That, Right? I'm Not Crazy, Right?

You know, there's something utterly captivating about watching a cat react to the world around it. I mean, have you ever seen a cat dart away from a harmless, everyday object? It's like witnessing a tiny, furry superhero in action, except instead of saving the day, they're just saving themselves from the terrifying threat of a rogue sock. It's a spectacle that never fails to amuse me, and I find myself laughing out loud, sometimes even when I'm alone.

Take my cat, Whiskers, for example. The moment he spots something out of the ordinary—like a crumpled piece of paper or a rogue shoelace—his eyes widen to the size of saucers, and suddenly, he's a blur of fur, darting away as if a lion were chasing him. You'd think the paper was a dragon, breathing fire, the way he leaps off the couch. I can't help but wonder what's going through his little cat brain at that moment. Is he thinking, "Oh no! The paper is going to eat me!" or "This is it; my time has come!"

Just the other day, I was minding my own business, sipping coffee and scrolling through my phone, when Whiskers spotted a rogue dust bunny. Yes, a dust bunny! You know, those fluffy little creatures that seem to multiply in the corners of your house when you're not looking. He crouched low, his tail twitching like a feather in the wind, and then—whoosh! He was off! I've never seen a cat move so fast. It was as if he was training for the Cat Olympics, and the gold medal was at stake. He leaped off the coffee table, knocked over a lamp, and then ricocheted off the wall before disappearing under the couch.

And let's not forget about the vacuum cleaner. Oh, the vacuum cleaner is the arch-nemesis of every cat. The moment I pull it out of the closet, Whiskers goes from zero to a hundred in less time than it takes to say, "Where's my cat?" He starts with a low growl, a warning sound that says, "I see you, you monstrous beast." Then, as soon as I flip the switch, he's gone. Poof! Like a magician's trick, one second he's there, and the next, he's vanished into thin air. I imagine him hiding in a closet, plotting his revenge, determined to take down the vacuum one day when it least expects it.

And don't even get me started on the dreaded cucumber. You know, that classic internet phenomenon where you place a cucumber behind an unsuspecting cat, and they leap into the air as if they've seen a ghost? I tried it once—just once—and let me tell you, Whiskers' reaction was a mix of disbelief and sheer terror. He took off like a rocket, knocking over the plant in the process, and I swear I could hear him thinking, "Why is there a green snake in my house?!"

What's truly fascinating is that it doesn't even have to be something that makes sense. I once watched him bolt away from a harmless cardboard box. A BOX! The very thing that's supposed to be his sanctuary, his fortress, his ultimate hideout. But no, the moment he saw it move slightly—thanks to a draft, mind you—he acted as if it were a portal to another dimension. He dashed across the room, and I couldn't help but laugh.

At the end of the day, I realize that Whiskers is just embracing his inner drama queen. Every little thing is a potential threat, and every ordinary object is a source of excitement. It's a reminder that sometimes, we need to find joy in the simplest things, even if it's just a piece of paper or a curious cucumber. Life can be chaotic and unpredictable, but if a cat can turn a mundane moment into an epic adventure, maybe we can too. So here's to Whiskers and his never-ending quest to escape the horrors of everyday life, one random object at a time!

https://app.videogen.io/view/grmtgu

Sneering And The Modern Housecat

You know, there's something about cats that's just inherently ridiculous, isn't there? I mean, take my cat, Whiskers. He's not just any cat; he's the embodiment of feline superiority, with a sneer that could make a seasoned diplomat reconsider their life choices. I swear, if cats had a governing body, Whiskers would be the president, and his campaign slogan would be, "Why bother?"

Every morning, as I stumble out of bed, bleary-eyed and clutching my coffee like a lifeline, there he is, perched on the windowsill, surveying his kingdom. The sun hits him just right, casting this angelic glow that would be downright enchanting if it weren't for the fact that he looks like he's judging my very existence. I can almost hear his thoughts: "Look at this human, shambling around like a lost sock. I could have caught a mouse by now."

And let's not even talk about the sneer. Oh, that sneer! It's like he's got a PhD in condescension. You know that look your mother gives you when you forget to take the trash out for the third time? Multiply that by a hundred, and you've got Whiskers' signature expression. It's a mix of disdain and disbelief, as if he's pondering the sheer audacity of my life choices. "You fed me that brand of cat food again? Really? You do know I have standards, right?"

It's not just the sneer; it's the timing. The other day, I was trying to do yoga in the living room, attempting to find my inner zen, and there he was, casually draped over my yoga mat like it was the world's most comfortable throne. I tried to shoo him away, and he just looked at me, one eyebrow raised, as if to say, "You think I'm moving for you? Please, the last time I did that, you put me in a carrier and took me to that place with the weird smells and the poking."

And let's not forget his impeccable timing when I have guests over. There's nothing quite like the moment when you're trying to impress your friends with your cooking skills, and suddenly Whiskers decides it's the perfect time to strut in, tail held high, and plop himself right in the middle of the dining table. He looks around like he's hosting a royal banquet, and I'm the jester trying to entertain the court. "Oh, you're serving pasta? How quaint. I prefer my meals with a side of judgment, thank you very much."

You know what really gets me? The way he manages to communicate pure disdain without uttering a single word. It's a skill, really. I'll be sitting on the couch, binge-watching my favorite show, and there he is, curled up next to me, but with that sneer plastered across his face. It's like he's silently critiquing my taste in television. "You call this entertainment? I'd rather watch paint dry."

And then, of course, there's the classic cat move: the slow blink. You know the one. It's like he's trying to communicate something profound, but all I can think is, "Is this a sign of affection, or are you just trying to hypnotize me into giving you more treats?" I blink back, hoping to establish some sort of connection, but he just sneers harder, as if to say, "Nice try, human. You'll never understand the depths of my superiority."

So here I am, living with a furry little tyrant who sneers at my every move, judging my life decisions like a furry little Simon Cowell. And you know what? I wouldn't have it any other way. Because in this bizarre world of cat-human dynamics, I find a strange comfort in the knowledge that, despite the sneering and the condescension, Whiskers is still my favorite little dictator.

https://app.videogen.io/view/wdsezs

Gravity Is A Cruel Mistress

You ever notice how cats have this innate ability to knock things off tables? It's like they've been training for it their entire lives, and the rest of us are just here to provide them with a constant supply of ammunition. I mean, we've all seen it. You're sitting there, minding your own business, maybe sipping a cup of coffee, and then out of nowhere, there's your cat, perched on the edge of the table like a furry little overlord, plotting your demise. And then, with the grace of a ballerina and the precision of a demolition expert, they casually swat at your favorite mug. It's as if they're saying, "Oh, you thought that was secure? How quaint."

I've often wondered what goes through their minds at that moment. Is there a little voice inside their heads saying, "I'm going to knock this off and watch the world burn"? Or do they think they're just playing some high-stakes game of Jenga, where the stakes are not just your coffee but also your sanity? I can just imagine them in a little cat council, discussing their tactics. "Alright, team, today we're focusing on the coffee cups. They're fragile, they're valuable, and they make a delightful sound when they hit the floor. Everyone ready? On three! One... two... three... chaos!"

And let's not even get started on the variety of objects they choose to send plummeting to the floor. It's like they have a checklist. "Hmm, should I go for the expensive vase that Aunt Edna gave you? Or maybe the stack of important papers you've been meaning to file? Oh, I know! The remote control! That'll really get them riled up." It's as if they have a secret mission to disrupt your life, one carefully placed item at a time.

You'd think they were trained by some covert military operation, but no, they're just house cats with a penchant for destruction.

And then there's the aftermath. You're left standing there, mouth agape, staring at the shattered remains of your favorite mug, and your cat is sitting there, looking completely unfazed. They're grooming themselves, as if to say, "What? That wasn't me. I'm just a fluffy little angel." And you can't help but feel like you're the crazy one for getting upset. I mean, who gets mad at a cat? It's like getting angry at a toddler for throwing a tantrum. You know it's going to happen; you just didn't expect it to be your prized possessions on the receiving end.

Sometimes I wonder if they do it for the attention. "Look at me, I'm a cat! I can make you yell! I can make you clean up broken glass! I can make you question your life choices!" It's like they're performing a stand-up routine, and we're the captive audience. "And next up, I'll knock over your laptop! Watch as they scramble to save their work while I act completely innocent! Ha! Comedy gold!"

But let's be real; there's something oddly charming about their antics. They bring a certain chaos to our lives, a reminder that not everything needs to be perfect. Sure, your mug is in pieces, and your heart might be a little bruised, but in the grand scheme of things, it's just stuff. And at the end of the day, it's a small price to pay for the joy of having a furry little creature that thinks it's the ruler of your domain. So, here's to the cats, the little tornadoes of fur and mischief, the masters of table-toppling. May they continue to knock over our coffee cups and remind us that life is too short to take too seriously, even if it means sweeping up the remains of our shattered dreams... and mugs.

https://app.videogen.io/view/tqgweb

Vanity of Vanities, All Grooming Is Vanity

You know, there's something truly fascinating about watching a cat groom itself. I mean, if you've ever had the pleasure of observing this ritual, you'll know it's like watching a master at work, a tiny fur-covered Picasso creating a masterpiece of cleanliness. It's as if they've taken it upon themselves to be the world's foremost authority on hygiene, and frankly, I'm here for it. But let's be real, there's a fine line between grooming and full-on obsessive behavior, and I think my cat may have crossed it.

First of all, let's talk about the sheer dedication. I'm convinced that my cat has a PhD in grooming. I'll be sitting on the couch, minding my own business, and there she is, licking her paw like it's a fine vintage wine, savoring every moment. It's like she's trying to extract the essence of her own fur. I can't help but wonder if she's thinking, "Ah yes, today I shall focus on the left hind leg. It hasn't received the proper attention since Tuesday!" And then, of course, she'll switch to her right leg, as if it's a whole different project requiring a completely new approach.

Then there's the technique. Have you ever seen a cat groom itself? It's a performance art form. One moment, they're licking their paw with the grace of a ballet dancer, and the next, they're contorting their bodies in ways that would make a yoga instructor weep with envy. I mean, how does she even reach that spot behind her ear? I've tried to stretch like that, and I ended up pulling a muscle. Meanwhile, my cat is just there, licking away, as if she's practicing for the feline Olympics. I half-expect her to score a perfect ten for flexibility and dedication.

And let's not forget about the noise. It's not just a quiet lick here and there; oh no, it's a full-on symphony of slurps and smacks. It's as if she's trying to communicate with the universe through the sounds of her own grooming. I can't decide if she's just really into her own cleanliness or if she's trying to send a message to all the other cats in the neighborhood: "Look at me! I'm fabulous! I'm the cleanest cat in town!" I can almost picture her standing on a soapbox, waving her paws in the air, shouting, "Grooming is next to godliness, my friends!"

But the real kicker is when she's done. You'd think she'd take a moment to bask in her own glory, admire the shine of her fur, and perhaps even take a victory lap around the living room. Nope! Instead, she plops down on the floor as if she's just run a marathon, and you can see the exhaustion in her little eyes. "What a day," she seems to say, "I've really outdone myself this time." And then, almost immediately, she's back at it, licking her tail like it's a gourmet meal that needs to be savored. I can't help but wonder if she's actually grooming or just trying to distract me from the fact that she's been plotting world domination all along.

But I guess we can't fault her for wanting to look good. After all, in the world of cats, appearance is everything. If you're not the shiniest, fluffiest creature in the room, what are you even doing with your life? So here I am, watching my cat, who clearly has a better self-care routine than I do, and I can't help but feel a little envious. Maybe I should take a page out of her book. I mean, if I devoted as much time to grooming as she does, I'd probably be a lot more put together. But then again, I'd also probably be licking my own elbow, and that's a whole different level of self-care that I'm just not ready for.

https://app.videogen.io/view/nzwkvm

We Climb Mount Furniture Because It's There

You know, there's something inherently comedic about a cat climbing furniture. It's like watching a furry little ninja in action, except instead of stealth and grace, you get a clumsy, chaotic display of acrobatics that would make even the most seasoned circus performer raise an eyebrow. I mean, have you ever seen a cat attempt to scale a bookshelf? It's like witnessing a poorly executed heist in a heist movie where the thief is both the mastermind and the bumbling fool.

Picture this: you're lounging on the couch, sipping your coffee, and suddenly you hear the unmistakable sound of claws skittering against wood. You glance over, and there's Mr. Whiskers, a majestic tabby with delusions of grandeur, eyeing the top of the bookshelf like it's Mount Everest. He crouches down, tail twitching with determination, and you can almost hear the theme music playing in his head. "I will conquer this mountain!"

He launches himself with all the grace of a potato falling off a counter, and for a split second, you think he might actually make it. But then, just as he's about to reach the summit, he miscalculates his leap, and instead of landing triumphantly on the top shelf, he crashes into a stack of books, sending them flying like confetti at a New Year's Eve party. It's a disaster, but it's also hilarious. You can't help but laugh at the sheer absurdity of it all.

And let's talk about the aftermath. Mr. Whiskers, now looking slightly dazed, sits amidst the wreckage of your favorite novels, as if he's just come back from a battle with a dragon. He licks his paw nonchalantly, as if to say, "What? I meant to do that." Meanwhile, you're left wondering if you should check on the books or just let them lie there as a testament to his failed expedition.

Then there's the couch. Ah, the couch—the ultimate feline playground. You'd think it would be a straightforward climb, right? Wrong. Cats have this uncanny ability to turn the simplest of tasks into a full-blown Olympic event. Mr. Whiskers approaches the couch, sizing it up like a contestant on a reality show, contemplating his strategy. He paces back and forth, tail flicking in agitation, and you can almost see the gears turning in his little feline brain.

Finally, he makes his move. He leaps onto the armrest, but instead of gracefully settling in, he misjudges the distance and ends up doing a dramatic faceplant into the cushions. It's like watching a toddler learn to walk for the first time. You want to laugh, but you also feel a pang of sympathy. He shakes it off, though, and with a newfound determination, he scrambles up the back of the couch, looking like a furry mountain climber reaching for the summit of K2.

And let's not forget about the inevitable "oops" moments. Cats are notorious for their lack of spatial awareness. One minute they're perched precariously on the edge of a shelf, and the next, they're tumbling down like a cartoon character off a cliff. You brace yourself for the thud, and when it comes, it's almost comical. They land, look around as if they're assessing the damage, and then strut away, tail held high, as if to say, "I meant to do that."

In the end, watching a cat climb furniture is a reminder that life doesn't always have to be serious. Sometimes, you just need to sit back, enjoy the show, and appreciate the hilarity of it all. Because if there's one thing a cat teaches us, it's that even the most graceful among us can have a bad day—and that's perfectly okay.

https://app.videogen.io/view/zmdubm

Whiskers And The Tree Of Temptation

You know, they say cats are graceful creatures, born acrobats, the ninjas of the animal kingdom. But let me tell you, when it comes to my cat, Whiskers, the only thing he's mastered is the art of getting himself into trouble. The other day, I witnessed a spectacle that I can only describe as a feline tragedy, a comedy of errors that would make even the most seasoned slapstick comedian weep with envy. It all started when I decided to take a leisurely stroll in my backyard, a place I like to think of as my personal oasis, complete with a small garden and a towering oak tree that has seen better days.

So there I was, admiring my daisies, when I noticed Whiskers perched precariously on the lowest branch of the oak. He looked like a furry little statue, all puffed up and proud, as if he had just conquered Mount Everest. I thought, "How cute! He's channeling his inner lion." But, of course, the moment I turned my back to grab my phone for a picture—because what good is a cat in a tree if you can't post it on social media?—that's when it happened. Whiskers, in all his feline wisdom, decided that the branch he was on was far too boring. He needed a challenge.

So there he went, leaping to a higher branch, and let me tell you, it was like watching a slow-motion train wreck. He miscalculated the jump by a solid foot, and instead of landing gracefully, he ended up dangling from the branch like a piñata at a children's party. I swear, I could hear the collective gasp of the neighborhood as they witnessed his acrobatics. "Is he stuck?" I thought. "Oh no, this is going to be a whole thing."

Now, you might think that a cat getting stuck in a tree is a classic tale, one that has been told a thousand times over. But what happened next was nothing short of a Shakespearean drama. Whiskers, realizing he was indeed stuck, began to vocalize his plight. It started as a soft meow, a gentle plea for help, but quickly escalated into a full-blown opera. He was belting out notes that would make Pavarotti proud. "Meowwwwwwwww!" echoed through the neighborhood, and I half-expected the neighbors to come out with popcorn, ready for the show.

I stood there, torn between laughter and concern. Should I rescue him? Should I call the fire department? I mean, what kind of person calls the fire department for a cat? But as I watched him flail around, I realized that I was witnessing a moment that would go down in history. I could already imagine the headlines: "Local Cat Becomes Tree-Climbing Sensation, Fails to Stick the Landing."

After several minutes of his dramatic performance, Whiskers finally decided to take matters into his own paws. In an act of sheer desperation, he twisted, turned, and somehow managed to free himself from the branch. He plummeted—graceful, right?—and landed in a bush that was probably more forgiving than the ground. He emerged, slightly disheveled, with leaves stuck to his fur and the look of a cat who had just been through a war.

He sauntered back into the house as if nothing had happened, tail high, strutting like he was the king of the world. I couldn't help but laugh. Here was a creature who had just faced the great outdoors, battled gravity, and emerged victorious—yet he acted as if he had just taken a casual stroll in the park.

In the end, I learned something that day: cats may be agile, but they're also ridiculously full of themselves. And as for Whiskers? Well, he's still the same cat who thinks he's invincible, and I'm just waiting for the next adventure. Because if there's one thing I know for sure, it's that a cat in a tree is just the beginning of a much larger story.

https://app.videogen.io/view/xvqmow

Look What The Cat Coughed Up

You know, there's something that happens in every cat owner's life that I think we can all agree is a rite of passage: the moment your beloved feline decides to decorate your living room with a hairball. Now, if you've never experienced this, let me paint a picture for you. You're sitting on your couch, perhaps sipping a cup of coffee, minding your own business, when suddenly, your cat's body contorts into a position that looks like it's auditioning for a yoga class. You might think, "Oh, how cute!" But that's your first mistake. Because the next thing you know, your cat sounds like it's auditioning for a horror movie, and you're about to witness the most dramatic performance of its life.

Let's break this down. First, there's that low, guttural sound. You know the one. It's like your cat is trying to communicate with the spirits of the underworld. You think to yourself, "Is this a cat or a demon?" And just when you're about to call an exorcist, it starts to happen. The cough. It's a cough that reverberates through the room, echoing off the walls, and you can't help but feel a mix of sympathy and absolute horror. You're torn between wanting to comfort your poor creature and the primal instinct to run for cover.

Then comes the moment of truth. The hairball makes its grand entrance, and it's not just any hairball. Oh no, this is a hairball that looks like it has its own zip code. It's big, it's fluffy, and it's a color that you can't quite identify. Is it black? Is it brown? Is it a mix of all the colors of the universe? You stare at it, wondering how something so small can produce something so grotesque. You can't help but wonder if this is what the cat was plotting all along. "I'll keep them guessing," it must have thought. "They'll never know what hit them."

And let's talk about the sound. It's not just a cough; it's an opera of sorts. It's the cat's way of saying, "Look, I'm not just a pet. I'm an artist." The crescendo builds, and you brace yourself for the inevitable conclusion. It's like watching a car crash in slow motion. You know it's going to happen, but you can't look away. And when it finally does happen, you can't help but feel a strange sense of pride. "My cat is a performer," you think. "A true master of the art of hairball production."

Now, you'd think after the performance, the cat would feel some sense of relief, maybe a little gratitude, but no. Instead, it struts away like it just won an award at the Oscars, leaving you to deal with the aftermath. You're left standing there, staring at this fuzzy mound of regret, wondering how you're going to explain this to your guests. "Oh, that? That's just my cat's latest masterpiece. It's avant-garde."

And then comes the cleanup. You grab a paper towel, or if you're feeling particularly brave, a plastic bag, and you approach the scene like you're defusing a bomb. You're not just cleaning up; you're performing an intricate dance of disgust and determination. You pick it up, and there's that moment where you think, "I can't believe I'm doing this." But you do it anyway because love knows no bounds—even when it comes to hairballs.

In the end, you can't help but laugh, because really, what's a little hairball in the grand scheme of things? It's just a reminder that life with a cat is never dull. They might cough up hairballs, but they also bring joy, companionship, and yes, a little bit of chaos. So here's to our furry friends and their artistic endeavors. May their hairballs be plentiful, and may our laughter be even louder.

https://app.videogen.io/view/uiqgly

Walking A Cat: You Ain't Going Nowhere

So, I recently decided to take my cat for a walk. Yes, you heard that right—a walk. You see, everyone always talks about how dogs love to go outside, how they prance around like they own the neighborhood, tails wagging like little flags of joy. Meanwhile, cats just lounge around, judging us from the comfort of the couch. But I thought, why not turn the tables? Why not show the world that my feline friend can also enjoy the great outdoors? Spoiler alert: I was wrong.

I grabbed the harness, which, let me tell you, is not designed for cats. It's like trying to fit a square peg into a round hole, except the peg is a cat, and the hole is their dignity. I managed to wrangle my cat, Mr. Whiskers, into this contraption, and he looked at me as if I had just suggested we go skydiving together. The expression on his face was a mix of betrayal and confusion, like I had just told him that his favorite napping spot was now a dog park.

But I was determined. I opened the door, and as soon as Mr. Whiskers felt the breeze, he froze. I mean, completely paralyzed. It was like I had introduced him to his long-lost nemesis: the outside world. He stared at the grass as if it were a foreign planet, and I half-expected him to start taking notes. I gently tugged the leash, and suddenly, he was a statue. A furry, disgruntled statue. I had to coax him with treats, which was the first of many mistakes.

Finally, he took a step. Just one. Then he sat down. I thought, okay, this is fine. He's just taking in the scenery, right? Wrong. He was plotting his escape. After a few minutes of my gentle encouragement, which included a lot of "Come on, buddy!" and "Look! A leaf!" he finally decided to move again. This time, he darted forward, and I was yanked off my feet. I found myself tumbling forward, my dignity trailing behind me like a lost sock.

Now, let's talk about the leash situation. You know how dogs have this innate ability to understand the concept of a leash? Cats? Not so much. Mr. Whiskers decided that the leash was a suggestion, not a rule. He zigzagged, he spun, he rolled. At one point, I considered that perhaps he was auditioning for a circus act. I was the reluctant ringmaster, desperately trying to maintain control while my cat performed a series of acrobatics that would put any gymnast to shame.

Then there was the matter of other animals. A dog approached us, tail wagging, and I could practically hear Mr. Whiskers' heart rate spike. He puffed up like a furry balloon, eyes wide, and suddenly, it was like I was walking a tiny, angry dragon. The dog, bless its heart, was just trying to say hello, but Mr. Whiskers interpreted this as a declaration of war. He hissed, he spat, and I could feel the judgment of the dog's owner as they looked at me like I was the worst cat parent in history.

After what felt like an eternity—though it was probably only fifteen minutes—I decided enough was enough. We retreated back inside, where Mr. Whiskers promptly flopped onto the floor and resumed his position as the king of the castle. As I collapsed onto the couch next to him, I realized that maybe, just maybe, cats are not meant to walk. They're meant to reign from their thrones, surveying their kingdom from the safety of the window.

So, if you ever consider taking your cat for a walk, remember this: cats are not pets; they are rulers. And we? We are merely their loyal subjects, forever at their service—preferably from the comfort of the couch.

https://app.videogen.io/view/fxsnoa

Bathing A Cat: Death By A Thousand Slashes

You know, the first time I decided to give my cat a bath, I thought I was being a responsible pet owner. I mean, how hard could it be? Cats are supposed to be these graceful, elegant creatures, right? They're like the ballerinas of the animal kingdom, gliding through life with an air of sophistication. Well, let me tell you, that's a big fat lie. The moment I announced my grand plan to my cat, Mr. Whiskers, it was like I'd just told him I was taking him to a dentist appointment. You know that look they give you? The one that says, "You must be out of your mind"?

So there I was, armed with a towel, a rubber ducky for moral support, and a bottle of cat shampoo that I swear was designed by someone who had never actually bathed a cat in their life. I filled the tub with lukewarm water, which, by the way, is a temperature that exists only in the minds of humans. Cats have a built-in thermostat that goes from "I'm fine" to "What have you done to me?" in about two seconds flat.

I picked Mr. Whiskers up, and he immediately transformed from a cuddly ball of fur into a squirming, hissing, four-legged tornado of chaos. It was as if I had just announced that we were going skydiving without a parachute. I swear, I could feel his tiny little heart racing as I carried him to the bathroom. The claws came out, and I suddenly understood why people wear gloves when handling wild animals. I'm pretty sure I still have the scars to prove it.

I plunged him into the water, and that's when the real fun began. Mr. Whiskers made a sound that I can only describe as a cross between a feral growl and a foghorn. I'm pretty sure he was trying to summon the spirits of all the cats who had ever been wronged by humanity. He flailed like he was auditioning for a role in a horror movie, and I was the unsuspecting victim. Water went everywhere. I was drenched, the bathroom looked like a mini water park, and Mr. Whiskers? He was plotting my demise.

I grabbed the shampoo, and as I squeezed it into my hand, I realized I had made a grave mistake. The bottle was designed for a cat, but the amount of shampoo that came out was enough to wash a small elephant. I lathered it onto Mr. Whiskers, and he retaliated with a series of high-pitched yowls that could shatter glass. At that moment, I understood the true meaning of "cat-astrophe." It was as if I had declared war on a creature that had no intention of surrendering.

Finally, after what felt like an eternity, I rinsed him off. The look on his face was priceless. He was soaked, disgruntled, and utterly betrayed. I half-expected him to file a lawsuit against me for emotional distress. I wrapped him in the towel, thinking he might appreciate the gesture. Instead, he took one look at me, and I swear I saw the gears turning in his little feline brain. He shot out of my arms like a furry missile, leaving a trail of water and indignation in his wake.

As he darted around the house, shaking off water like a dog, I couldn't help but laugh. There he was, the epitome of fury and humiliation, and yet so undeniably adorable. I realized that giving a cat a bath is not just a chore; it's an experience, a rite of passage, a comedy of errors that will haunt you for years to come.

So, if you ever find yourself contemplating the idea of bathing your cat, just remember: it's not about cleanliness; it's about survival. And if you do decide to go through with it, maybe invest in a good pair of gloves and a first-aid kit. You'll need them. Trust me.

https://app.videogen.io/view/stwetc

Birds and Mice and Bugs Ought To Scurry

You know, there's something inherently majestic about cats. They prance around like tiny, furry monarchs, surveying their kingdom and demanding tribute in the form of treats and head scratches. But let's talk about their darker side—their role as the ultimate insect and rodent exterminators. I mean, if there were a reality show about cats, it would be called "Pest Control: Feline Edition," and it would be a smash hit. Picture it: a cat in a tiny hard hat, strutting around with a clipboard, checking off "mice" and "bugs" like they're on some grand to-do list.

Now, my cat, Sir Fluffington the Third—yes, I named him that; I thought it added a touch of class—takes his job very seriously. He's not just lounging around, acting like a fluffy overlord; no, he's on a mission. His first target? The common housefly. You know the type: buzzing around, thinking it's the life of the party, when in reality, it's just a nuisance. Sir Fluffington sits there, eyes narrowed, tail twitching with anticipation, like a seasoned sniper waiting for the perfect shot. And when that fly lands? Oh boy, it's like watching a slow-motion action scene. He pounces with the grace of a ballet dancer and the ferocity of a lion.

But here's the kicker: he never actually catches the fly. Instead, he lunges and misses, his paw swiping through the air like he's trying to catch a ghost. The fly, clearly unimpressed, buzzes away, leaving my cat looking utterly bewildered. It's as if he's just realized that he's not actually the apex predator he thinks he is. I can almost hear him muttering to himself, "Next time, I'll get it. Just you wait."

Then there are the mice. Oh, the mice. You'd think they'd learn to stay away from our house, given that Sir Fluffington has a reputation. But no, these little critters are either incredibly brave or just plain stupid. I once witnessed a mouse scurry across the kitchen floor, and Sir Fluffington's reaction was priceless. He froze, eyes wide, as if he'd just seen a celebrity. He crouched down, preparing for the hunt, but instead of launching into action, he started to play with a piece of string. I mean, come on! A mouse is literally a few feet away, and he's more interested in the string that's been sitting there for weeks.

Eventually, he did notice the mouse again, and that's when the real drama unfolded. He launched himself into the air, but instead of landing gracefully, he miscalculated and crashed into a chair. The mouse, probably laughing its tiny rodent head off, took off like it was in an Olympic sprint. Sir Fluffington, meanwhile, picked himself up, shook it off, and strutted around as if he had just executed the most magnificent leap in feline history. The only thing he caught that day was a bruised ego.

And let's not forget about the bugs. Ants, spiders, and those weird little beetles that seem to pop up out of nowhere—Sir Fluffington treats them like they're his personal playthings. I once watched him stalk a spider, and I was convinced I was witnessing the next great nature documentary. He crouched low, ready to pounce, and then... he got distracted by his own tail. I mean, who can blame him? It's fluffy and wiggly and just begging for attention.

So here's the thing: while he may not be the world's most effective pest control agent, he certainly provides endless entertainment. Every failed pounce, every bewildered look, and every moment of distraction adds to the joy of having him around. Sir Fluffington may not be catching any pests, but he's certainly catching my heart—and that's a win in my book.

https://app.videogen.io/view/mjujdg

A Simple 20 Page Manual On Petting A Cat

You ever notice how petting a cat is like trying to solve a Rubik's Cube while blindfolded? Everyone thinks they know the secret, but the reality is it's a chaotic dance of trial and error, punctuated by sudden claws and the unmistakable sound of betrayal. I mean, you'd think it would be simple, right? You approach, you extend your hand, and voilà – instant feline friendship! But no, my friend, it's a minefield of preferences, moods, and, let's be honest, a little bit of passive-aggressive behavior.

First off, there's the initial approach. You can't just swoop in like you're about to give a high-five to a toddler. No, no. You've got to channel your inner cat whisperer. You crouch down, hand extended, palm up, like you're offering a peace treaty. But here's the kicker: you've got to read the cat's body language like it's a Shakespearean play. Is the tail high? That's a good sign! Swishing? Maybe she's just getting her groove on. But if that tail's puffed up like a feather duster? Back away slowly, my friend. You're about to enter the danger zone.

Then there's the petting technique. Ah, the art of petting. It's not just about the strokes; it's about the rhythm. You can't just go in there with a full-on petting frenzy. No, that's how you end up on the receiving end of a swat that could rival a ninja's. You've got to start slow, gentle, like you're caressing the world's most delicate fabric. I've found that the best starting point is right behind the ears. It's like the cat's version of a spa day. But if you dare venture below the chin too quickly, you might as well have declared war. Suddenly, you've got a furry little dictator demanding respect for its personal space.

And let's not even get started on the "sweet spot." You know what I'm talking about. Every cat has that one magical place where they melt like butter on a hot day. For some, it's the base of the tail. For others, it's the belly. But here's the catch: if you find that sweet spot, you're a hero. If you misjudge the situation and go for the belly too soon, you're a fool. It's like trying to pet a landmine. One wrong move, and you're in a world of hurt, nursing a gash that could've been avoided had you just stuck to the ears.

And what about the purring? Ah, the glorious sound of a content cat. It's like music to your ears, right? But let's be real; purring can be misleading. You think you've hit the jackpot, and then, out of nowhere, the purring stops, and you're left wondering if you've just committed a cardinal sin. You try to retrace your steps, backtrack your hand movements, but it's too late. The cat has already decided you've crossed some invisible boundary, and now you're just a mere mortal in the eyes of a feline deity.

Now, let's talk about the aftermath. You've successfully navigated the petting process, and you're feeling like a champion. But then, out of nowhere, the cat decides it's time for a dramatic exit. One moment you're basking in the warmth of your cat's affection, and the next, she's leaping off your lap like she's just spotted a laser pointer. You sit there, bewildered, wondering what you did wrong. Did I pet too hard? Was my technique off? Did I accidentally summon the spirit of an ancient cat god?

So here's the takeaway: petting a cat is an art form, a delicate balance of intuition and finesse. It's a journey filled with unexpected twists, a few scratches, and a whole lot of laughs. So next time you find yourself in the presence of a cat, remember to approach with caution, pet with care, and always, always respect the feline code. Because at the end of the day, you may just be a humble servant in the kingdom of cats, and they're the ones who hold all the power.

https://app.videogen.io/view/yvushi

Dogs And Cats Confidential: Furry Frenemies

You know, they say opposites attract, but I'm beginning to think they just drive each other completely insane. I mean, take my cat, Whiskers, and my dog, Rufus. You'd think I was trying to blend oil and water, but no, it's more like mixing a tornado with a brick wall. Every day is a new episode in their ongoing saga of coexistence, and I'm just the hapless producer trying to keep the chaos from spilling over into my own sanity.

Let's start with Whiskers. She's the queen of the house, and she knows it. She struts around like she owns the place, which, to be fair, she probably does. I mean, I feed her, I clean her litter box, I even let her sit on my lap while I'm trying to work. But the minute Rufus walks in, it's like she's just spotted a raccoon in her garden. The hissing, the puffing up, the dramatic flopping onto the floor as if she's been mortally wounded. You'd think Rufus had just declared war on her royal highness.

And then there's Rufus, my lovable golden retriever. He's like a giant, furry bundle of joy wrapped in enthusiasm. Honestly, if he were any more excited to see me, I'd have to start charging him rent. But when it comes to Whiskers, his enthusiasm takes a different turn. Picture this: Rufus sees Whiskers lounging on the couch, and his tail starts wagging like it's auditioning for a part in a musical. He bounds over, tongue lolling, eyes sparkling with pure doggy delight, and what does Whiskers do? She leaps off the couch like she's just spotted a snake. I swear, she can jump higher than any Olympian.

The other day, I caught Rufus trying to sneak up on Whiskers while she was basking in the sun. I thought, "Aww, look at him trying to make friends!" But then I remembered that Rufus is less of a sneaky ninja and more of a clumsy elephant. He tiptoed over, all four paws stomping like a marching band, and before I could even shout, "Don't scare her!" he let out a bark that could wake the neighbors. Whiskers didn't just jump; she flew. I'm pretty sure she broke the sound barrier.

Now, you'd think after a few of these encounters, Rufus would learn to tread lightly, but no. He's got the memory of a goldfish. Every time he sees her, it's like he's just discovered a new toy. And Whiskers? Oh, she plays the long game. She'll sit there, pretending to be aloof, while plotting her next move. One moment she's licking her paw, and the next, she's launching herself off the bookshelf, landing right on Rufus's back. It's like a scene from an action movie, only with less coordination and more fur flying everywhere.

And let's not even talk about mealtimes. I've tried everything to keep the peace. I bought separate bowls, I feed them at different times, but somehow, it always turns into a scene from a reality TV show. Rufus will finish his food in record time, then look over at Whiskers, who's daintily nibbling on her kibble like it's a five-course meal. The next thing I know, Rufus is trying to shove his face into her bowl, tail wagging like he's just found the holy grail. Whiskers, of course, responds with a glare that could melt steel.

At the end of the day, I wouldn't trade this chaos for the world. It's like living with a sitcom, where the punchlines are always unexpected, and the humor is as raw as the cat hair on my couch. Whiskers and Rufus may never be best friends, but they've certainly made my life a lot more interesting. And honestly, who needs a boring household when you can have a cat and a dog trying to coexist? It's a comedy of errors, and I'm here for every ridiculous moment.

https://app.videogen.io/view/qkffnf

Also by Kevin Lawson

Drawn But Not Forgotten
The First Time I Ever...
The REAL College Survival Guide
The REAL High School Survival Guide
The Real Cat Owner's Survival Guide